Jonathan Li
Trafalgar Squ

C000092467

David Lines was born in Nottingham in 1967. He
has written for radio, magazines and newspapers
and has recently completed his first novel.

He is currently writing situation comedy for
network television.

The author lives in York.

John Abbott was born in Toronto, Canada, before
settling in the UK where he forged a career in
advertising.

He now works for a large agency in Yorkshire.
With a thirst for popular culture, John has had
several books published and is involved with a
number of media-based projects.

By the same authors

The XXXX Files
PMT

Jonathan Livingston Trafalgar Square Pigeon

David Lines

art direction by
John Abbott

ARROW

Published in the United Kingdom in 1998 by
Arrow Books

3 5 7 9 10 8 6 4 2

First published in the United Kingdom in 1998 by Arrow

Arrow Books Limited
Random House UK Ltd, 20 Vauxhall Bridge Road, London SW1V 2SA

Random House Australia (Pty) Limited
20 Alfred Street, Milsons Point, Sydney, New South Wales 2061, Australia

Random House New Zealand Limited
18 Poland Road, Glenfield, Auckland 10, New Zealand

Random House South Africa (Pty) Limited
Endulini, 5A Jubilee Road, Parktown 2193, South Africa

Random House UK Limited Reg. No. 954009

A CIP catalogue record for this book
is available from the British Library

Papers used by Random House UK Ltd are natural, recyclable products made from wood grown in sustainable forests. The manufacturing processes conform to the environmental regulations of the country of origin

Typeset in Optima
Printed and bound in the United Kingdom by The Bath Press, Bath, Somerset

ISBN 0 09 927839 1

'We're words upon a window
Written there in the steam
In the heat of the moment
Everything is what it seems
Vapors passing nearly
So I'm touched by the thought
That I can't be beaten
And I can't be bought'

'Heavy Soul (Pt 1)' by Paul Weller

DAVID LINES

I have been inspired by so many people in my life –
love and thanks to you all.

JOHN ABBOTT

Well, we did it. Thanks to everyone who I've mentioned
before, and a few more besides. 'Come with Uncle and hear
all proper. Hear angel trumpets and devil trombones.
You . . . are . . . invited!'

jon@alien23.demon.co.uk

'But some time or another you gotta get out.
Because it's crashing.
And all at once those frozen hours melt through
the nervous system and seep through the pores'

Bruce Robinson
Withnail and I

Part One

Above ground, it
was barely daylight, Jonathan Livingston Trafalgar Square Pigeon coughed up last night's excesses and beat his scratty little wings as fast as he could.

The need to travel at a speed probably greater than any other pigeon in London at that time was based solely on the fact that Jonathan was only seconds away from being rear-ended by the first tube of the day as it pulled into Swiss Cottage.

The forward draught created by the train served not only as a forewarning of its arrival to the few waiting commuters, but as extra and much needed propulsion to the poor pigeon. Just two or three inches in front of the driver, Jonathan summoned up all of his energy to speed him out of the tunnel.

Gasping for more air, he dipped three of his primary wing feathers downwards to bank hard left where he landed, knackered, on the platform to start hopelessly pecking at a half sucked Polo mint.

The cotton that bound Jonathan's feet and claws dug deep into his skin. The circulation had been cut off months ago, and it wouldn't be too long before one of his feet dropped off, too. But Jonathan was far from interested in the preening process. He lifted his cracked and fractured beak, pausing only to pick up a discarded condom before tossing it aside, off the platform and onto the rails.

Most birds, pigeons occasionally excepted, don't bother to ride the Tube. There's only a select few who have discovered the delights of Underground travel and even fewer who have mastered the knowledge required to cross the entire city of London without beating a single, battered wing. Jonathan Livingston Trafalgar Square Pigeon was one such bird.

Jonathan was not like other pigeons, that much is true. The acceptable face of modern day pigeon life stemmed from years and years of tradition that included posing for photographs with tourists, sitting on people's heads and Caking the Column. But these things simply were not enough for this bird. They were too much like hard work and nowhere near exciting enough to hold Jonathan's interest for very long.

The bird's parents had lambasted him for travelling on the Tube and the sting of parental disdain had smarted enough to deter Jonathan from doing so, whilst simultaneously focusing his activities on regular pigeon life. 'Don't you see, Jonathan?' asked his father, not uncaringly. 'Your life is here with us, where we belong – not underground. If your destiny lay below The Square, you'd have brown fur and a curly, pink tail. But you don't – you have feathers!'

So Jonathan tried very hard to be a normal pigeon, concentrating on flocking together with the other birds and growing fat on the bread that swelled in his crop and was forever being flung in front of him. As Jonathan stood and stared down at the bread at his feet he could feel the vibrations of the underground system, coursing up through his grey, feathered body and terminating at his very soul.

The need for speed was within him forever and the pigeon quickly tired of this uninspiring existence. Before long, Jonathan was pulling funny faces at the tourists' cameras and yearning for some fun in his life.

It was no good, the lure of the Tube drew him more and more with each passing day. There was another world, and it was directly beneath him every minute of every day. Jonathan Livingston Trafalgar Square Pigeon stood at the top of the stairs that lead down to the tube and took a long, deep breath. His heart felt like a bomb going off, and it was with much glee that Jonathan hopped down the steps one at a time before standing in awe and staring up at the map of the Tube, savouring the act of choosing where to travel to that day.

Where to go! The choices were overwhelming – red line, blue line, yellow line or the brown line – which one?

Truth be told, it didn't really matter much. But, wait! That was the past and this was now. There had to be rhyme and there had to be reason to this new life. There had to be a purpose; and then, suddenly, it was inside Jonathan's mind like a cartoon idea complete with light bulb appearing

overhead! Despite the bedazzling choice of destinations plastered on the wall before him and the pigeon picking randomly at names – he would visit every single one! Genius! No more for Jonathan the impossible task of opting for a stop. Instead, the task, the project, the Mission became so pure and clear. There was no need to take to the air ever again. Why would there be? The pigeon never left London – didn't need to. All of the humans used the Tube, they had no use for flight – so why should Jonathan? And all of these destinations! Just look at them! What names! – Parson's Green, Chalfont and Latimer, Burnt Oak, Mudchute and the delightful Heron Quays.

'There's no time like the present, Jonathan,' the bird said to himself. 'It's like being a boy in a sweetshop. Right, I'm going to Charing Cross and it's on the Northern Line. Or is it the Jubilee Line? Or the Bakerloo Line? Good grief! It's on three lines!' Decisions, decisions. 'Confusion should rein below ground, but it doesn't. I've so much to learn.'

The bustle of both tourist and commuter carried on around him as the grey bird busied himself with plotting the journey back to Trafalgar Square.

'Swiss Cottage is on the grey line, and if I follow this route from here and then get off at Charing Cross then I'll be back at the Column.'

The bird was strangely drawn in the direction of the

focal point that is the very epicentre of pigeon life. Not out of any real feeling of belonging to his feathered breathren, but to show them his achievements; his discovery of District Line and Central, Jubilee and Northern, East London and Circle and all the others.

The familiar forward draught from within the tunnel came once more, and the people on the platform picked up their briefcases and baggage in readiness for its arrival. The bird roused itself and stepped closer to the edge, more sure of securing a seat for the journey.

None of the other passengers-to-be could feel it, apart from this pigeon. Even though his feet were far from being in the best of condition, Jonathan's claws picked up the not too distant rumbling of the connection as it careered towards its next stop. And here it came; lights and noise and electrics and metal and grinding and fast and then slow and stopping and then still.

Jonathan braced himself. He knew what was coming, and every time he heard the words they sent a shiver through his quivering feathers. 'Be still, my quills,' he thought. 'Say it! Say it!'

'Mind the gap.' Heaven.

Doors opened, quietly. With only four other passengers waiting at Jonathan's carriage, there would be no problem with seats.

The bird was wary of being trampled underfoot and decided to get on before the other passengers.

And first on he was. But not without having to beat his wings just once. 'Technically speaking, that does not constitute flight. My body did not leave the ground for a period of time long enough to qualify as flying. It was a flap-assisted jump – or am I just kidding myself?'

The woman who sat opposite Jonathan on the train took up all of the space on either side of her seats with bundles of dirty, worn carrier bags. The print on the plastic advertising the store from which she bought (more probably, found) them had almost entirely disappeared. She was large in size, and wore three pairs of musty support tights to insulate and protect against the elements. The pigeon stared at her impressive whiskers and less impressive blackened teeth until the jolt of the Tube pulling away brought him back to earth.

Nobody gave the bird anything more than a cursory glance as he travelled with them that morning. 'Next time, I'll bring a pen and a copy of *The Times*. Let's see just how unimpressed they all are when I start doing the bloody crossword…'

The motion from left to right and back again, coupled with the hot blasts of air from the heaters under the seating, made Jonathan very sleepy very quickly, but he fought against it and made a mental note to get hold of a Walkman through which he could listen to his favourite songs and annoy passengers at the same time. 'That'll keep me awake, alright.'

How could his fellow birds fail to appreciate the joys of the Underground? How could that be? Surely all that flapping around and unnecessary exercise was entirely uncalled for in today's modern world of gadgets and gizmos. How long had this wonderful system of underworld travel been down here? Who was responsible? Which magnificent architect of such vision sat down and drew up this heaven below ground? Jonathan could only marvel at the achievement. And then he sprayed a jet of watery white shit up against the seat.

'Wonder what the fine for that is?'

Screwing his eyes up, Jonathan physically willed the Tube train to go even faster, wishing for it not to bother stopping off at the stations between there and Charing Cross – his message was of the utmost importance! His message was one of hope and discovery! It must be delivered to the Elders as swiftly as possible. By turning their backs on flight they need not worry about cold and wet and rain, frosts, sleet, gales and snow! No cause for concern regarding tourists with their clicking cameras. Nor would they ever have to worry over whether or not the restaurant men would come for them during the night. 'Hurry, train, hurry! Carry me back with my message of hope!'

The pigeon stared up at the map above the opposite window and his brain wrestled with the number of remaining stops before he had to change lines.

'Where you going then, work?' the voice laughed.

Jonathan looked up. It was the bagwoman, smiling down at him. 'Where I'm going and by the time I'm finished, no pigeon will ever have to work again,' he replied, full of pride. The bagwoman reached down into one of her bags and pulled out an individual fruit pie, minus the tiny silver foil tray it once sat in. She carefully removed the lid whilst the bird watched maybe a dozen grains of granulated sugar drop down onto the floor below. 'Want some pastry, little pigeon?'

'No, not now, not ever again. From here on I'll never accept any more food from humans in exchange for entertaining them. This idiot woman obviously finds me amusing,' thought Jonathan, 'and in my book, pastry equals payment.'

The bagwoman had, thankfully, shut up and was happy to simply slurp the fruit pie's filling through the lid. They were now at a point on the Jubilee Line midway between Baker Street and Bond Street. With only two stops left, Jonathan could barely contain his excitement and cooed quietly to himself at the prospect of putting his case for a no-flight policy to the pigeons and Elders.

The train moved on through Bond Street and Green Park, and Jonathan was suddenly only two minutes away from Charing Cross.

They would be so proud of him! The pigeons would adore him forever! With the gift that he brought them, surely the name of Jonathan Livingston Trafalgar Square Pigeon would live on in the minds of his fellow birds forever and a day. He had a vision of pigeons evolving to the point where they would have so little need for flight that their wings would actually cease to work. One day a bird would be born without wings – it would carry nothing more than a travel pass. The burden of airborne horseplay would be put behind birds forever and… 'Enough of this daydreaming! Get off at the next stop and go forth and spread the word, that no pigeon need ever again debase itself for the titillation of tourists.' To do this, they must free themselves from the trap of Trafalgar Square – and with that would come a new, easier life free from flying. How they'd applaud him – Christ, they might even build a statue in Jonathan's honour for all of the tourists to come and crap all over.

And there it was! The sign on the tiled wall next to a weird cream and white mural – Charing Cross. Time to deliver the sermon. And off Jonathan got. Through the doors, turn left and onto the escalator. Nice one.

It was of enormous, continuous surprise to Jonathan that he never had the living shit kicked out of him by human

passengers on the Underground. Either by mistake or on purpose. Oh, sure, he'd been booted a couple of times – but only in really busy situations, and, as far as Jonathan could tell, never on purpose. Injuries sustained so far had amounted to two broken claws and a blow to the side of his head that actually made him see stars! But, hey! That was modern life for the modern pigeon and they'd all have to take the knocks at first to get used to it. There was going to be a new world order – and flight for pigeons in the capital would soon be over. Fight the good flight.

To take to the air and fly across the road to The Square would have been the final insult, and walking through traffic was an unnecessary hazard this close to delivering the plan. The bird concentrated hard on the signage and homed in on the types of passenger most likely to be heading there, too. He needn't have tried so hard; the force that drew him to The Square was too strong to even try and ignore. And before he knew it, Jonathan was there amidst ten thousand pigeons. To tell them never to fly again.

The days of discovery that lay ahead for Jonathan and the flock seemed full of anticipation.

By the time Jonathan came up out of the subway steps, the flock had been gathered together in a loose semi-circle for some time. Waiting. The day was bright and crisp and the pigeon seed stall was doing a brisk trade with tourists happily pelting the pigeons to within inches of their lives using the brittle grain and shiny husks of seed as both nutrition for the flock and ammunition against it. Nobody seemed to be eating very much, and the birds eagerly tightened the semi-circle as a hush fell amongst them.

'Jonathan Livingston Trafalgar Square Pigeon! Stand to Centre Square!' The words spoken by the Elder could mean only one of two things. Standing to Centre Square was only ever called for when dishonour or praise were to be dished out. 'Such high praise to be bestowed!' thought Jonathan. 'Truly, they are to join me forever below ground! To be followed is one thing, but it's not praise or accolade I want (although I still quite fancy the idea of an enormous statue…), just to share my vision with everyone else is enough!'

The Elder repeated his command, interrupting Jonathan's daydream. 'Jonathan Livingston Trafalgar Square Pigeon! Stand to Centre Square!' Puffing his pigeon chest outward and raising his head skyward, Jonathan Livingston stepped forward to take the Centre Square. Waves of pride washed over him, bathing him in a warm, gushing glow.

'Jonathan Livingston Trafalgar Square Pigeon,' called the Elder. 'Stand Centre Square for shame in sight of your fellow pigeons.'

The words struck him like a blade in an alley. They cut just as deeply and the pigeon's pride poured from the wound.

Centred for shame? No way, man! The Underground – they've got it wrong – there must be some mistake!

'...for this bird's flagrant abuse of the laws of The Square,' the harsh voice continued, clipping his wings and, ultimately, his ticket, 'abusing the laws and traditions of the Pigeon Family...'

To stand centre for shame had always, and could only result in one thing – expulsion from The Square.

History showed Jonathan Livingston that those who had gone before him, banished from the focus, ended up the other side of London in somewhere like Neasden. The horror ran through his feathers with a chilling pain.

'Oh my God.'

'Jonathan Livingston, you have been warned – repeatedly – of the dangers and embarrassment and ridicule which you seem hellbent on bringing to the Family by riding the Devil's Worm. No more shall we tolerate this insolence. Begone!'

He wanted to reply to his Elder, but to state his case would appear only as answering back to the Family. Why couldn't they see that The Square trapped them, that it was the tourists who were guilty of humiliating the pigeons? This young bird did not want to travel by Tube on his own – he wanted to share this joy, this release from being nothing more than an attraction. To speak back to an Elder would mean that whatever hope Jonathan Livingston had of being spared banishment would go up in smoke as soon as he stepped forward to open his beak to speak back to an Elder.

None of the Family had noticed the little girl with the red balloon and the funky star-shaped sunglasses standing with her parents. Their three-day stay in London was the second leg of their whistle stop UK tour. 'Mummy, Daddy! See how I make them fly!' The girl ran straight towards the flock, the balloon trailing behind her. There was maybe sixty or seventy feet between them.

The Elder continued.

'Go, now. Leave The Square and find, if you can, your own misguided way. Flight is the gift we have bestowed upon us and by turning your back on this beauty you turn your back on us all…'

Jonathan's voice faltered as he addressed the Elder.

'You are all of you so very, very wrong! The world is changing, London is changing and as it changes, so should we! We can break away from the confines of The Square and discover the delights of this great city without ever beating a single wing. We are as much a part of London as the Underground, in fact we were made for each other! Join with me and travel the Tube, free from this circus we have created for ourselves!'

London Underground

A collective gasp went up from the Family and as it did, so the birds did, too. Thousands of wings lifted them high up into the air to avoid the rocketing child as she tornadoed on through the birds and brought her right foot down, entirely unintentionally, on top of the Elder. Her sandalled foot crunched on his body, squashing his innards so that they spewed out from under her. The girl's parents swooped down to whisk her away just as her tears came, and as they came so did the Family – back to form the semi-circle around Jonathan.

The death of the Elder caused nothing more than a murmur amongst the birds. With so many Elders, the next in command took control and continued the speech.

'Just go. Jonathan, just go…' But Jonathan interrupted, 'Look for yourselves, see what the tourists bring you? Death is their gift…'

Jonathan could see it really was useless. Dead eyes stared back at him from all around. He turned to leave. If he couldn't take them with him, then he wasn't going to miss out himself.

Jonathan Livingston Trafalgar Square Pigeon had stood trial and been banished. The family turned their backs on him forever, whilst on a more personal level, Jonathan Livingston fancied a spot of Seven Sisters.

Hope soon returned to his heart and Jonathan Livingston revelled in his new life. He soon learned to recognise all of the lines by name, not just by colour, and with every passing day began to use his wings less and less. And the escalators! Such heaven! To climb high and then to come back down! Without flight! Oh, this was the life, this was the London life! With smoking outlawed on the Underground, there was never any embarrassing pecking at platform food only to discover that it was a fag end, like all other pigeons did. To aimlessly travel from one end of the city to the other was all that this bird had ever wanted to do, and now here he was, living his life to the full.

If the other members weren't going to follow him, then bollocks to 'em, thought Jonathan Livingston.

It was about half past four on a wet Tuesday afternoon when they appeared, and found Jonathan alone in a carriage on the Circle Line squatting over a discarded copy of Razzle. The four pigeons that came into the carriage and sat down next to him were as fat and lardy as Jonathan Livingston could ever wish to be. The largest bird had lost both of its feet and was roughly the size of two pigeons rolled into one. The other three birds were all equally out of condition and the smallest bird was missing an eye.

'And...?' asked Jonathan.

'And what?' replied the fat bird.

Jonathan Livingston sighed. 'And what do you want?'

'We want to help you, that's what.'

'Oh God, look – if you're part of some weird sect or something pervy like that then you can just piss off,' said Jonathan.

The pigeons smiled back at him before answering.

'No, we are here to spread the word for you. To take you under our wing, so to speak.'

'Oh please,' said Jonathan Livingston.

'Politeness is a virtue long forgotten in this world,' the one-eyed wonder chipped in, smiling.

'Look, just piss off, right? You're all really weird. Go away, go on, piss off.' And Jonathan got off at Stamford Brook.

The train pulled away and Jonathan Livingston waddled across the platform to wait at the other side for the next train. Frankly, he didn't much care where it was going to, as long as those freaks weren't on the Tube. The familiar rumblings of an approaching connection vibrated up his pink legs, but this time it felt different. Jonathan had always been able to tell not just when there was a Tube pulling in long before it did, but how far away it was, too. But not this time.

As if by magic there appeared before him a silver tube train, bathed in a calming ethereal light, its arrival made even more spectacular by the sound of a thousand heavenly choirs piped through the platform P.A. system.

'Bugger me,' said Jonathan, as one of his claws dropped off.

The door of the train opened silently and the heady aroma of roses filled the pigeon's nostrils. Jonathan didn't exactly step onto the train; he was carried on board by the feelings of goodwill and love that spilled out onto the platform from within.

Hovering before him was a pigeon the size of a labrador. The enormous bird must have been a good three feet off the ground and it hovered alright, but not in the same way that your average kestrel does. This bird wasn't even beating its wings. It was just... floating there. This enormous pigeon had dressed in long, flowing golden robes and although lacking the pink-eyed signature of albinos, its feathers were glowing a brilliant white.

'Welcome, friend,' boomed the pigeon.

'Sod off,' replied Jonathan. 'You're doin' me head in.'

The decor inside the carriage was far from standard issue. Instead of maps of the Underground, old masters took their place. Where straps and springs should have hung, there were plush red bellropes and the worn, tattered cloth seating had been replaced by chesterfields and rocking chairs. The 'room', as it were, was entirely in white, emitting warm, comfortable feelings of a dizzying bliss.

'Christ, Network South East have come on a bit,' said Jonathan.

'Alas, not. I'm afraid that privatisation has yet to yield enough of an upgrade for splendour such as this,' replied the gigantic floating feral pigeon. 'You, my boy, are about to take a trip in the Train of Thought...'

Part Two

LITTER

Jonathan didn't need

a ticket to ride the Train of Thought, no sir. All that was required was for him to close his crusty eyes and… think. And when Jonathan thought of a place, he was there! There in his magic train. Piccadilly Circus, Parsons Green, Putney Bridge or Park Royal; all he had to do was just wish. The Train of Thought transported Jonathan to wherever he wanted to be! Sometimes the Train arrived on the track in just a blink of an eye. Sometimes it hovered above the rails and occasionally it had to wait for the train in front to leave. When Jonathan wanted to visit a place of interest to tourists, like Marble Arch or Leicester Square, then the Train would emerge from the ether above the Underground, suspended a hundred feet in the air. Looking down on the masses.

Of course, the Train was invisible to everyone other than those travelling within and on the whole things went smoothly. Sure, there was the odd hiccup; like the incident which resulted in a singularly messy shunt out at Ongar. But that's another story. And then there was that sorry tale in Sudbury Hill, and then the unmentionable happened in Mornington Crescent. But, on the whole, life underground had been great fun. So Jonathan was really surprised when on a trip way out near South Wimbledon, the Magic Train of Thought just, well… stopped.

Its speed reduced quite rapidly and they were obviously drawing to a halt. The pigeon wracked his brains, trying to remember if he'd made a wish to make the stop, but he hadn't. Jonathan Livingston peered out of the window, which wasn't too difficult as he was sitting on top of an enormous white bean bag at the time. There, waiting on the platform were three beautiful birds. Feral pigeons; trim, lithe and proud in stature, they stared up at the traveller, their eyes brimming with hope and spilling over with love. But who were they? Jonathan Livingston hadn't authorised this stop. Up until now, Jonathan Livingston Trafalgar Square Pigeon had believed that he, and he alone, controlled the Train. But if it wasn't him, then who was driving it?

'Greetings, Pigeon. We are your friends; here to travel with you through good times and bad. Let us continue this journey together, marvelling at all which the world has to offer.'

'Oh Christ. Not more hippies,' said Jonathan. 'Sit down. I'm gonna find out who's driving this thing…'

Jonathan Livingston jumped down from his beanbag, brushed past the intruders and made his way through the buffet car towards the front of the train.

Jonathan was spared the usual lack of 'something to eat' on what he considered to be his special Tube train, in that this one did indeed have a buffet car. And a coop. And a lovely, heated preening parlour. Further along the carriages one could find other delights, including a seed vending machine, bird bath and a fascinating contraption that appeared upon first glance to be a shoe buffing machine rather like those normally found in hotel corridors. In actual fact the device operated in a very similar manner to the shoe shine machine, but was meant instead for the de-tangling and removal of cotton from the feet of pigeons. Really, this place was heaven.

Just as Jonathan Livingston was making his way toward the front of the train, it juddered to a halt, throwing him across the passageway – the bird fought hard to stop himself from taking to the air to avoid impact with the wall – but only just. Despite the severity of what felt like a collision of some sort, Jonathan had sustained no real damage bar a set of very bent tail feathers. 'Bugger. Oh well, I'm due for a moult, anyway.' Picking himself up and rousing his feathers, he found his bearings. 'Right. First things first. Got to find out just what the Devil's going on with yet another unscheduled stop. Now, window…'

Jonathan Livingston waddled at top speed back toward his beanbag and, using his beak as a mountaineer uses a pick, butted it down onto the linen and levered his way slowly up. It was hard work on the old shoulders and the ascent took the best (or worst) part of a minute. By the time he'd reached the top, he bloody well wished that he hadn't.

For some reason that to this day remains utterly unexplained, the Train of Thought had pulled into, and stopped at, Bromley-by-Bow.

'Dear God! What in the name of sweet Wanstead are we doing here?' When Jonathan Livingston scanned the platform his little leathery heart turned to stone and the sight before him made his feathers stand, quite literally, on end.

Standing on the platform were five of the most enormous feral pigeons he'd ever set eyes on. Hooded pigeons, masked in black. As the doors opened automatically, swishing back like a garden spade schlicking up through wet mud – they were inside. This was not good.

Jonathan remained where he was, pretending to himself that if he remained still they wouldn't spot him, move on, get off and that all would be well again.

But it wasn't. Far from it.

These guys weren't armed, that was the first thing that Jonathan Livingston noticed. But then he realised, quite quickly, that they didn't need to be. They had a presence that was far more intimidating than facing whatever weaponry they could have been packing.

Smooth and silent in their actions, the pigeons glided on board looking from left to right with an air of professionalism which instantly told Jonathan Livingston they'd done this before.

The first two set off down the train, through the carriages, checking where the passengers were, how many of them were there, and then herding them back down the train, confining the startled ornithoids all together into a manageable area.

Having established that the carriages to the front of the train posed no problem in terms of any vigilante birds, the remaining intruders jostled Jonathan downtrain to join the group. Jonathan Livingston and his brids were very aware that this situation was potentially explosive. This group of intruders all shared the same wing markings, their plumage dappled black and grey with a central white splash on each shoulder. Some just displayed the one snowy dot, others two and the leanest, fittest pigeon with four circles.

'Attention! Eyes front!'

Jonathan cast a glance out of one of the windows to check their location. The train hadn't moved.

'You! What did I say? Look-at-me!' With that, one of the one-spot birds smashed out his right wing, driving it into Jonathan's face. A cut opened above his eye and blood blobbed onto the bird's downy cheek feathers.

'Ow!' thought Jonathan.

'Ow indeed!' thought his attacker.

'Wait a minute – he's not speaking,' said Jonathan Livingston.

'No. I'm not. I'm thinking to you…'

When nothing more than a young squab, Jonathan Livingston Trafalgar Square Pigeon would sit in the nest with his tiny body squidged up nice and snug and listen to the stories told by his father. There were many different tales, mostly of the Square and how it came to be and of those who came to see, to stand and stare and feed the birds, and the bird would listen to those words with warmth and love and child-like glee. But of all those golden, mystery tales there was one which echoed through the nestling's head long, long after the story finished. Closing his eyes, he would rewind his father's words, play them back and savour each and every one. It was always the same story which he listened to over and over, and that was of the pigeons who lived together so closely and loved each other so much that speech became redundant and the power of thought was the all-seeing, all-speaking communicator. Just by smiling at one another the make-believe birds showed their love, and it truly was felt by all.

But this group of terrorists had harnessed that power! The gift of telepathy which Jonathan Livingston had only ever dreamt of was real! It was here in all its power and all of its glory but, by God, it wasn't being used for the good of love – but for evil.

The leader continued, 'Jonathan – step forward.'

He did so, and stared this monster straight in the eye.

Without opening his beak, Jonathan Livingston addressed the despot directly.

'Look, man. This is a Love Train, the Train of Thought and, you know, we're just ridin' it to wherever we feel like goin'. Go and find your own train. Von Ryan's Express this is not. We really don't need any of these bad vibes – that's why we're here. We're running away from all of those bad vibes – correction – we have run away from that shite which confines us to everything that's expected of us. You stomp in here togged up to the nines in this para-military clobber and expect me to offer you tea and biscuits? Bollocks!'

The pigeon hit Jonathan so hard that his beak fell off.

Of course, none of Jonathan's troop had heard a word of this exchange – which made the blow to him all the more shocking for them.

The beak on the floor didn't help much, either.

As for speaking, that was pretty much a non-starter, too.

'If I'm gonna talk to these pigeons – and I've got to – so that they know just what the hell's going down, then I'll just have to try and think really, really hard. If these ruddy terrorist pigeons can use telepathy, then my guys must be capable.'

'No they're not,' thought the leader.

'Listen, you. What's your name? More importantly, what's your bloody game?'

The leader slipped him a sly smile and stood on one leg to scratch behind an ear. Rousing his plumage slightly and then taking three steps forward, he was barely half a beak length away from Jonathan Livingston's face. He could almost taste his captor's breath, it was that foul, and the air exhaled from the nostrils cooled the wound where Jonathan's beak used to be. A droplet of blood fell from it onto his foot, snaking itself around the outline so that when Jonathan stepped back one pace to avoid the halitosis he left a bloodied claw outline, reminding the pigeon of chalk marks around a body which he once saw on TV through the window of a branch of Radio Rentals in the Edgware Road. It was an early episode of Columbo, but Jonathan wasn't to know that.

Closer now, he went on, 'My name's Colonel Latimer.' You could have knocked Jonathan down with a feather. Of course! That was it! Latimer was the name of a pigeon banished a few years before Jonathan Livingston had hatched; dismissed by the Elders along with a handful of other birds for flagrantly flouting the Rules of The Square. 'These other guys must be the rest of them…'

'…and allow me to introduce my comrades; they're men of wealth and taste – Colin Dale, Infantrybird Perry Vale, Sergeants Stan More and James Park and this is my Captain, Russell Square.'

It was them! Well known throughout birdlife folklore, this bunch had a reputation – and it wasn't for helping little old pigeons across the street.

'What you have to understand, little bird, is that unlike some dreadful B movie, we do not possess a list of manic, hair-brained revolutionary demands that includes such tedious items as money, arms, hostage releases, that sort of stuff. What we demand, and believe me – what we're going to get – is total control of this Train of Thought. Yes, we've hijacked it and yes, it's ours. You've seen the force that we're prepared to exercise. The unorthodox removal of your beak was, granted, an unfortunate loss but beware that it was only the beginning. A casualty of war…'

'No matter. I'll grow another one.'

Latimer laughed a little, 'That's the spirit, lad. That's the spirit.'

Sergeant More yelled at the Infantryman, 'Vale – eyes right! Wheel in the weapon! On the double!'

'Sir!' and off he flew, down the carriage.

Jonathan looked at Latimer and thought, 'Weapon? What's the weapon all about?' Then asked, 'Come on, it's not as if we've put up much of a fight, right?'

'True, your resistance has been far from remarkable, but we have to be sure of success. Anyhow, we may well need it when we arrive at our ultimate destination. How's your beak? Hurts?'

Jonathan crossed his eyes trying to focus on where it used to be.

He looked quite ridiculous.

'That's sweet of you to ask. It's hurting like a bitch, now that you come to mention it. I think the wound's clotting quite nicely, though.'

Latimer reached out with a primary wing feather and gently stroked his wound. 'Don't look so hurt, child…'

'I am hurt. You knocked my sodding beak off…'

'Well, there is that, I suppose.'

A low rumbling sound broke up their discourse as the pair of pigeons turned to face whatever was making it. And what was responsible for the guttural grinding revealed itself as truly a weapon of great destruction. To pigeons, that is.

No larger than a jar of coffee, the weapon vaguely resembled one, too. Protruding from the front was a barrel about five inches in length and rather thin in its diameter in relation to its reach. Strawish, I suppose. A red button on its side flashed repeatedly on and off. A low-pitched humming noise came from within it.

Everyone gathered around the device to get a closer look.

'Not too close, my friends. Not too close, now.'

Jonathan was right in fearing the worst.

Infantryman Perry Vale stepped away from it, nodding once to Stan More.

'Good work bird. Keep an eye on this crowd.'

'Don't worry, Sir. Anybird tries anything, and me and Big Bernice'll let 'em have it good and proper.'

Jonathan moved a little closer to it. 'Big Bernice?'

'Don't laugh. This blighter'll bring you down at seventy feet.'

'Scary. But what is it?'

Latimer narrowed his eyes and lowered his voice. 'This high-tech, state of the art piece of devilry is a Foot Binder! Armed with three hundred and fifty feet of the deadliest cotton produced, it's accurate to the point of lunacy. There's no escape once it's got you in its sights. Tight, cutting and potentially lethal. This thing'll take a foot off as soon as look at you. Any questions, gentlemen?'

They all shit themselves and took four steps back.

'No.'

'Good. That's that sorted, then.'

Jonathan spoke next. Drawing himself up to the bird's full height and puffing out his chest, and raising the obvious question, 'O.K., so where do you want to go to in the Train of Thought? Where will it take you?'

And the bird looked at Jonathan. 'Oh, no. Don't think you're getting off that lightly. In fact, you're not getting off at all. And as for details of our destination I thought you would know that, in your heart.'

Jonathan guessed it in his head.

'That's right. Set the controls for the heart of The Square! Trafalgar Square, here we come!'

When Jonathan Livingston Trafalgar Square Pigeon left The Square, he'd promised himself that he'd never return. Banished forever into what the Elders termed the Wilderness, the bird had found a new life full of hope and dreams that was free from the restraints of pandering to tourists' needs – and it was a good life, with a pioneering spirit, and for this he was eternally grateful. But to go back? To return had never been an option. No way.

But this? Under the direction of another? This bird couldn't go back without at least some semblance of a fight. And anyway, it was Jonathan who was in control of The Train. They couldn't make him take them there. Could they? So what, they've got this cotton binding gun – he'd already had the living shit kicked out of his beak. What's a couple of lost feet between friends, anyway? No, he'd do his best to fight against this lunacy. But why did these terrorists need to be back at The Square? Why?

Still not used to having his own mind read, Latimer answered Jonathan's question soon enough.

'Your train is now under the control of the P.L.O.'

Jonathan glanced across Big Bernice at him. 'Really. And that's what, exactly?'

'The Pigeon Liberation Organisation, you dumb schmuck.'

Ignoring the pain from his wounded face, Jonathan let out a burst of laughter that set all of the hippy pigeons off, too. He fell to the floor of the train and clutched his fluffy white undersides, such were the convulsions of hysteria.

'You will take us seriously, idiot!' yelled Latimer.

Choking back the funny side Jonathan Livingston asked why.

'Haven't you learnt anything? For the selfsame reason that you left.'

'But if you think it's that bad back at The Square, then why return?'

Latimer composed himself, replying, 'The Pigeon Liberation Organisation are returning with a mission, and the mission is to free all pigeons of the needless, worthless rulings which bind the birds to the never-ending task of entertaining tourists in a demeaning, ridiculous manner. When we're back there – and you are coming with us, our primary task is to

overthrow the Elders, remove them from The Square and take control for ourselves.'

'A military coo, then.'

'Very funny. Shut up and listen. Actually that is funny. Anyway, the P.L.O. will help instigate a series of mini councils that are run entirely autonomously in a democratic, non-authoritarian state for the good of the birds and no-one else. *Capiche*?'

'*Si.*'

'Why are we talking Italian?'

'You started it.'

'Sorry. Look, this is the point where if you actually had a choice, I'd tell you that you're either with us or you're not. But you don't have a choice so sit down and behave. You're a big bird, but you're out of condition and I do this full-time. Sit tight while I see a man about a dog.'

Latimer motioned towards Captain Russell Square who reached down into a kit bag and pulled from it three porcelain struts. The last of them was slightly obscured from Jonathan's view by Big Bernice's barrel, but it appeared to be a familiar shape. Very quickly, the two of them set about assembling the components.

'On the double, Square – I'm bursting!' cried Latimer.

There, before Jonathan, was a scale replica of Nelson's

Column. Latimer flapped up onto Nelson's head and, with a sigh of relief, relieved himself down the side of the effigy.

'That's better,' he oozed.

'What the…'

'Don't ask, Jonathan. It's a psychological thing.'

So he didn't.

Having been separated from the New Age Pigeons who had been carted off to some distant compartment at the other end of the Train of Thought, Jonathan Livingston was now confined to barracks in a rather swish sleeper, complete with four poster nesting box, bird bath and seed dispenser (gilt edged, very nice).

Reclining in the box, he couldn't escape the nagging question of who exactly was in charge of the Train. If it had stopped without his express wishes then there must be somebird else at the helm.

Next task was to break out of there and get to the driver's cabin – pronto.

'Oh, no,' thought Jonathan, 'I suppose I've got to act like a man for once…'

The first problem facing Jonathan was one that faces us all, and that was of the unknown. What exactly was unknown to the ornithoid was, who was outside guarding him? Latimer's henchmen armed with the Cotton Binder was the worst that it could get. Jonathan Livingston could take a beating – but he didn't need another. As for his pink, scaly feet bound forever in cotton, that was another matter. The only way out was through the sliding doors, unless… compromise. That was an answer. In fact, that was *the* answer. If the pigeon could somehow manage to get out of the window then he could totally avoid whatever guards were there, on his way to the driver's cabin. But – and the 'but' was a big 'but' – Jonathan Livingston Trafalgar Square Pigeon, the bird who'd made a stand and vowed never to beat a single wing ever again – would have to – *fly*.

Well, we all have to bite the bullet sometimes. Question that remains is how to get out of this window… Brushing aside his worries to avoid the problem of Latimer being capable of reading his mind from any distance, the bird began to survey the window. The glass had got to be, by his estimations, at least five millimetres thick. Realistically, there was no way in this world (or the next, come to that) that he could smash it. Even a fracture was way beyond this bird. 'Sod it,' he thought. 'Come on, man – apply yourself!'

Pecking was out of the window. You need a beak for that, not a bloodied cavity.

That left scratching and clawing. With one foot? This situation got worse. How in the hell was he supposed to deal with this conundrum? What was he, a magician? No.

Or was he?

Come on, now. If Jonathan Livingston had it in him to teleport a train from one end of London to the other and back again, then surely it couldn't be too difficult to wish himself ninety feet to the other end of this bloody thing.

Could it?

Well, my friends, it was worth a try.

And in the best traditions of fairytales he had a go.

Magic. Oh, yes. That was the stuff. Like Doctor Who's Sonic Screwdriver or Superman's amazing powers, magic acts just the same as a 'Get out of Grief Free Card', and, in the best traditions of make believe it invariably works.

But not for Jonathan.

Not on his first attempt, anyway.

Or his second, or his third.

Or his thirty-seventh, come to mention it.

'Maybe I'm wishing in the wrong way,' he asked himself. 'It worked for that other bird when his back was against the wall. You know, that seagull dude...'

The pigeon sat down in the corner, put his wing up around his face and splayed the feathers to hide his frustration.

You bet. And as if by magic the seagull appeared!

Here we go, thought Jonathan Livingston. There's magic at work.

'Jonathan Livingston Trafalgar Square Pigeon, you find yourself in a regrettable position, my boy. That much is true. But you took your lead from my previous antics many decades ago. You're in a scrape, and we can't change the past – but you can learn from it. So far you've mocked me with tongue firmly embedded in your cheek – but, hey, I forgive you. You wanted to do something radical, just like me. Before all of this you were nobody – nothing! But to break away is the only love worth fighting for – and I get the feeling that you're something of a trooper when it comes to this. Now, I can help you if you look closely at my past. But don't mock me. Sure, come browse in my library and check out my wardrobe, come to me as a healer and I'll help cure you – but only if the medicinal requirements are all there; dine in my restaurant and think in my tank, cook in my kitchen and sleep in my bed – but if you piss in my swimming pool then for heaven's sake don't blame me when you swallow some water. O.K.?'

'Er… no.'

'What?'

'Actually, yes. Please get me out of here!'

The gull smiled sweetly and reached out to place a comforting quill on the shoulder of his protégé.

'O.K. I'll forgive you. You're young and naive. To find your own path you firstly need to follow someone else's. Just so happens that this time it's mine. The old always give way to the new and –'

'– Just get me the hell out of this carriage!'

'Ahhh, the impertinence of youth. And all that stands between you and the truth is a window. Funny how the most difficult obstacles always appear so clearly…'

The seagull slowly turned his neck backwards and held the pose, whilst managing a knowing wink to Jonathan. A word to the wise, if you like. The blur of his beak travelled at a speed that would surely have gone unregistered, way off the scale of instrumentation designed to measure such things (you know, like a beak impact velocity computator or something).

The gull's beak connecting with sheet glass at this velocity sounded like a high-powered rifle going off in your ear. But twice as deadly. Shards of glass flew everywhere, tiny glistening splinters of danger speeding through the air. Man, there was so much of the stuff! The shrapnel rained down on them, sounding as it did like a lunatic let loose in timpany heaven. An orchestra conducted by Glass… and with that the gull was no more. Gone forever. And when the tinkling ceased the pigeon looked on up and, lo, the window was no more! Free!

'Right, son. It's your move. Get out of here before the guards rumble you, get down to the driver's carriage and find out exactly who's responsible for your destiny – because you can be sure it isn't you!'

It had been a while since this bird had flown. He'd grown fat, true to his wishes. His wing muscles had flabbed out and gone to seed and the two beats that it took to carry him up onto the window ledge left the pigeon gasping for air.

And with one bound, Jonathan was free.

He launched himself upwind of the train, in the direction of the secret driver. The wind sliced through the wound on his face and he had to gulp back the pain and just try and fly through it. Which he did with great bravery. It felt like the bird was gagging, choking back the air as it rushed into his nostrils, sped down the pigeon's throat and ballooned his tiny lungs which felt as if they were soon to burst. Dipping down low over the platform, the forward draught was reduced somewhat, though the pain didn't go away. It couldn't have been more than a hundred and twenty five (human) feet, but the distance seemed like a marathon, burning and pushing Jonathan Livingston to his very inner limits.

That said, the act of flying was a surprisingly thrilling one for him, and the sneaky feeling of regret crept up on Jonathan, tapped him on a blue, feathery shoulder and reminded him of the one thing he'd turned his back on but which, of course, he'd been born to do.

Never an Olympic medallist in the flying department, this short but incredibly painful flight was becoming more and more enjoyable! 'Could I have been wrong to never fly again? After all, you only miss what you've taken for granted when you don't have it anymore,' he said to himself. How true.

Sixty feet and counting. The bird was closing in. Craning his neck and lowering his shoulders, this most popular of moves helped him drop down another twelve inches to enable real low-level flying no more than a foot from the ground.

'Look at me – I'm airborne!'

Nobirdy heard him, but it didn't matter. This bird had a mission, and it was drawing to a close. A sorry, sorry close.

Thirty feet now, and still closing fast.

Perhaps too fast, as Jonathan hadn't planned for what he was actually going to do once he got to the cabin. 'Confrontation, now that's not my forté,' he said, words lost in the wind behind the bird.

As is often the case when one's back's up against the wall, the questions come thick and the answers even faster.

'Where's my beak gone to?'

'Will I really make it to the end of the train without collapsing in a bloodied, knackered heap?' and 'Who's in there? What happens if there's six of 'em, and I really do end up having the crap beaten out of me?'

And then the BIG question came back into his brain, rapping on the front door of Jonathan's mind like a deranged collector for Help the Aged demanding receipt of the bin bag pushed through your letterbox seven weeks ago and expecting to have the thing handed over, stuffed to the brim with roll neck sweaters and cardigans that your uncle gave you way back.

'Who's in charge of your destiny? Who's in charge of your past, present and future, bird? Tell me who it is that's driving this thing and, ultimately, your life! Go on – tell me who it is!' It wasn't really the kind of question one could particularly ignore very well, but, like most pigeons of his generation, he did so.

Five feet left. Time to land.

Not the most gracious of landings. Truth be known, if a bystander had witnessed it, said manouvere would have been more likened to a wet slipper falling off the roof of a car than one of God's beautifully designed creatures swimming through the air and coming expertly to rest.

But that's Jonathan for you…

And there the bird was. Three feet away from all of the answers which all of us, at sometime or another, truly seek.

'Now you're stuffed, me laddo.'

Turning to his right Jonathan came face to face for the second time with the famous gull.

'Hey, thanks for sorting out that window situation, man. You've got one hell of a beak on you!'

And the gull looked at Jonathan.

'That's why I'm here for you, kid. If you really do mean to discover the secret of everything, well, first you'll need to get in there. Thought I'd lend a hand with breaking the glass again. Stand back, bird.'

'Really, that's very sweet of you, Gull, but I reckon I've no need for your help, now. What'cha say 'bout the old giving way to the new? Time's up, Seagull. Fly away, old timer…'

With that Jonathan stepped forward, flapped up and butted the 'Press to Open' switch, swathed in red light on the outside of the driver's cabin. Blood sprayed out in two tiny but powerful jets from his beakless nostrils and 'Schikk!' the electric door slipped to one side and he was in.

'Here we go, Jon. The Moment of Truth.'

Shockingly calm given the gravity of his situation, Jonathan took three very cautious paces into the cabin. Such a brilliant white light blinded him, taking the bird some

F.P.I. FEATHERALL PIGEON INVESTIGATIONS

TRAFALGAR'S MOST WANTED

DO NOT APPROACH THESE BIRDS - THEY ARE BOTH A NUISANCE AND A HEALTH HAZARD

COLONEL LATIMER

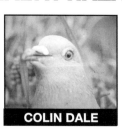

COLIN DALE

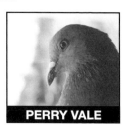

PERRY VALE

STANLEY MORE

JAMES PARK

RUSSELL SQUARE

TO
MAJOR GENERAL
SIR HENRY HAVELOCK
K.C.B.
AND HIS BRAVE COMPANIONS
IN ARMS
DURING THE CAMPAIGN IN INDIA
1857

seconds to blink away the ethereal aura of it all. A hundred thousand cellos sounded through the air and for a moment he thought he recognised the crescendo from Bach's Sarambande for the Cello Suite No.1 in G. But then again it could well have been cries of ten million souls falling into the abyss.

No matter. Ho, hum.

The cabin was much smaller than he'd pictured it. A huge Lloyd Loom chair (high backed) faced away from the door. So much white; the room appeared to have been recently decorated although there wasn't a paste board nor a tin of paint 'with a tint of' (anything) to be seen.

The music was still present, acting like a drug to soothe the pigeon's now almost non-existent anxieties. So calm and so coolly focused, he moved through the heavenly environment taking in the pictures on the walls which included many Old Masters and a potato print signed 'Alice, aged nine years and three months'. 'Cute, real cute,' he thought.

To the left of the chair was a table set for dinner. Draped in a white cloth which had been yanked to one side, the table featured a pair of candlesticks – one which was lit and the other fallen onto its side, extinguished.

'Man, this is too heavy,' thought the pigeon. 'Just too heavy…'

As our bird approached the table he could spot more features. There was a bowl of fruit; white, fine bone china with crisp, green apples, a banana, grapes, peaches and something exotic from Sainsbury's which Jonathan didn't recognise. 'Sophistos,' he said to himself. An orange whirred, too, but to that he paid no notice.

Coming up behind the chair he could hear heavy, laboured breathing. Heart beating faster, the calm giving way to panic, almost. Rushing over and through his soul, Jonathan pushed away the adrenaline and rounded on the chair's occupant.

'Oh – My – God...'

He could actually feel the answers to everything now. There they were, ready to reveal all.

The pigeon wondered why nobody had prepared him when he was younger for life like it was really going to be. Why didn't the teachers at school ever sit him down and drive home what the future would actually throw at him? He didn't know, so Jonathan Livingston Trafalgar Square Pigeon turned and faced his nemesis.

It was another pigeon. Roughly the same build as Jonathan, but with perfect feet and the shiniest hue to its plumage. Healthy, muscular and sweet-smelling – this was a pigeon with a difference, though.

The bird wore a mask moulded from white plastic. Just

like a theatre mask, though not smiling nor sad – just a long slit that stretched from one side to the other. Jonathan crapped himself.

The masked ornithoid sat in front of what looked like a bank of controls. Flashing buttons of red, green, orange and gold blinked on and off in no particular sequence, and the control panel also housed a number of levers, switches and huge dials.

'What is this?' Jonathan Livingston asked of the mystery bird.

Nothing – absolutely nothing in reply. Just a nondescript blankness from the mask.

'Why are you here? What are you doing? This is my train! You can't drive this – get out!'

Nothing. The faceless bird stared back at him.

'Say something! Speak to me! What are you doing here?'

Nil. Zero. When it came to reactions and replies the cupboard was bare.

Unable to contain himself any longer, Jonathan Livingston lunged at the pigeon and drove his claws into its mask. Ripping the cover away, he revealed another mask. This was rubber, moulded into the guise of a ginger, Cheshire Cat. The grin that sneered back at Jonathan was too hideous to bare. Again he lunged forward, and again he connected. Snatching the cat mask away, this time it revealed a circus clown – hideously painted in a leering laugh that was just too much; again he cast it aside. Clawing frantically now and experiencing no resistance the bird went on to reveal a rat, then a mouse followed by a city gent in a bowler hat.

Tears of rage ran down his face as the next mask proved to be a seagull followed by a judge with a wig. Next to be thrown aside was the policeman and then the face of his father, Jonathan's father.

'Stop this! Stop this! Show me who you are! You must, please…'

Crumpled at the leg of the chair, Jonathan raised his head to face his controller.

And the face which stared down at him came as no shock to the bird.

The face that greeted him was finally revealed as the face of the very entity which had for so long trapped and guided him; both plotting and scheming against him whilst simultaneously pretending to have only Jonathan Livingston Trafalgar Square Pigeon's very best interests at heart.

And the face that stared back at the bird was that of himself.

'You!'

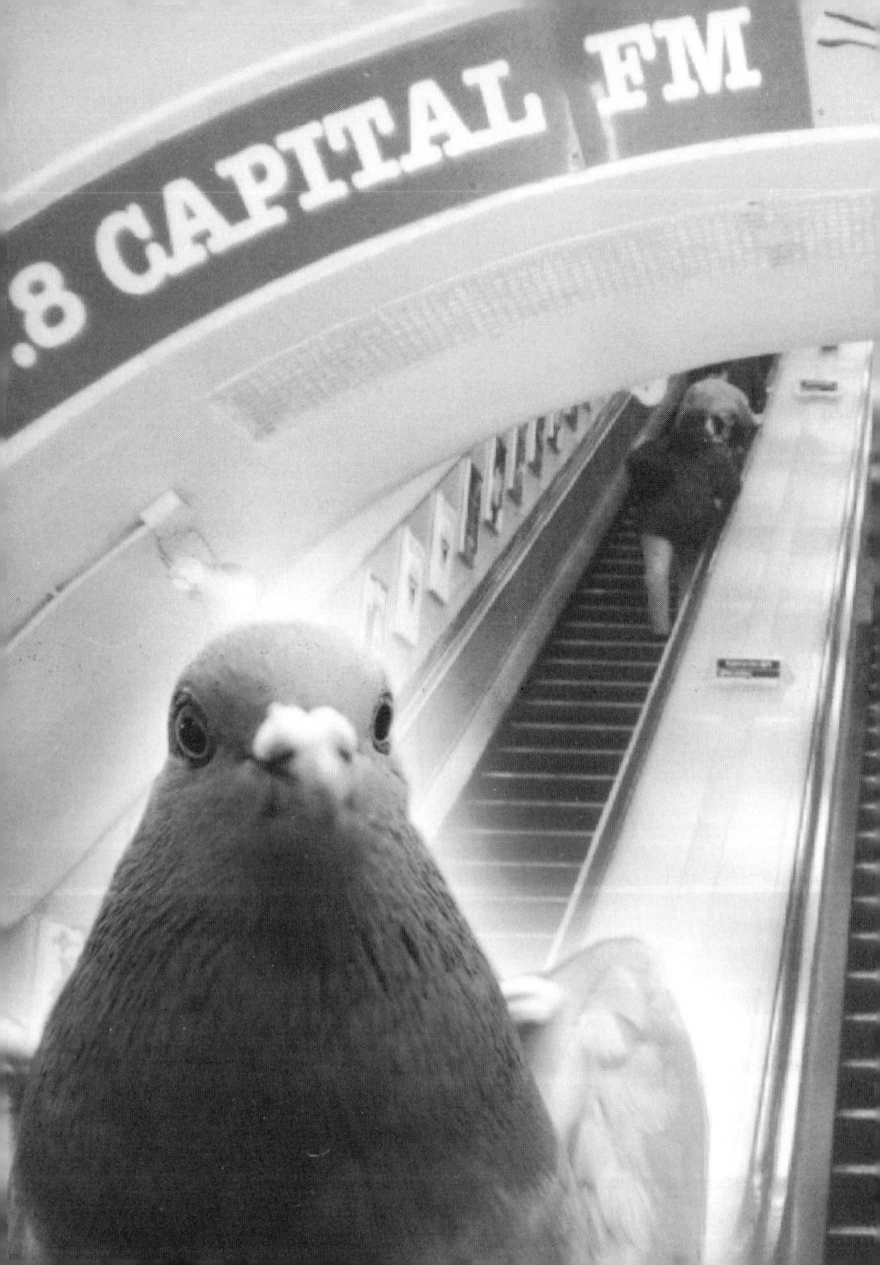
.8 CAPITAL FM

'Yes, it's me. It has been all along, you fool!'

The truth had been so obvious and the bird should have seen it coming like a train down a track. He was his own captor – had been all along. Bound only by his own inhibitions and prejudices, the wall of self-doubt and disbelief had been built by himself. Shrouded in secrecy for so many years up until now, the truth reared its head and laughed in Jonathan's face.

'To know our own destiny is the only path that our lives could ever take, and you never even knew yourself. How could you possibly hope to lead others when you shunned the true you? You idiot! Jonathan, you know what you must do. And if there's a second chance for you after all of this, then learn from your mistakes, and should the opportunity ever arise again, then look inside yourself for the answers – search for the true you!'

Bloody hell.

'Sanctimonious tosser!' and with that, Jonathan hit himself so hard he almost felt it, too. The alter ego fell backwards, catching his head on the table's corner and rendering the bird unconscious.

It was all so clear, so beautifully clear. Still the tears rained down on Jonathans face, his heart pounding so loudly that he felt ready to explode.

Instinctively taking the controls, Jonathan pressed three

buttons and turned a green dial clockwise as far as it would go. He pulled hard on a lever, and finally produced the desired result: the Train of Thought came to life.

Mechanisms whirred, the engine stirred, juddering a little, and then, with a jolt, and a cock and a snook at all that this world had brought him – they were away!

The harder Jonathan pulled back on the lever, the faster the Train travelled.

Train track turned to wide, open countryside and the blur of grey switched to the swathes of green. In only seconds, the Train moved from being motionless to travelling at the speed of light – and beyond.

As the terrible machine passed over the coast, Jonathan looked out of the window and saw a boy on a scooter, parked on the edge of the cliffs. The lad's parka blew in the southerly breeze, his hand revving the throttle of his bike. Clutch in, then out – Jonathan pulled hard on the lever, all the way back at exactly the same time and then… there was nothing. The train kissed this world goodbye before disappearing forever in a big, loud bang. Whatever would greet those commuters in the key of life was anybody's guess, but five'll get you ten it was far better than that which they'd left behind.